Stella Brite
and the
Dark Matter Mystery

WITHDRAWN

Sara Latta

Illustrated by Meredith Johnson

ini Charlesbridge

For Tony, Alison, Caitlin, and Eli. With all my love.—S. L.

For Bailey and her little brother Chad—M. J.

Grateful acknowledgment is given to the following experts:
Charles Alcock, Harvard-Smithsonian Center for Astrophysics
John Arabadjis, Massachusetts Institute of Technology's Kavli Institute
for Astrophysics and Space Research
Tony M. Liss, Physics Department at the University of Illinois
Harry Nelson, Physics Department at the University of California, Santa Barbara
R. Bruce Ward, Harvard-Smithsonian Center for Astrophysics

Credits: page 9: NASA; page 26: NASA/MIT/J. Arabadjis et al.
Text copyright © 2006 by Sara Latta
Illustrations copyright © 2006 by Meredith Johnson
All rights reserved, including the right of reproduction in whole or in part in any form.
Charlesbridge and colophon are registered trademarks of Charlesbridge Publishing, Inc.
Published by Charlesbridge, 85 Main Street, Watertown, MA 02472
(617) 926-0329 • www.charlesbridge.com

Library of Congress Cataloging-in-Publication Data
Latta, Sara L.
  Stella Brite and the dark matter mystery / Sara Latta ; illustrated by Meredith Johnson.
    p. cm.
  Summary: Stella and her brother, Max, of the Brite and Brite Detective Agency, put the mystery of
Mayor Pickle's missing Pekingese on hold as they join the astronomy club in researching the problem of
invisible dark matter in the universe.
  ISBN-13: 978-1-57091-883-4; ISBN-10: 1-57091-883-X (reinforced for library use)
  ISBN-13: 978-1-57091-884-1; ISBN-10: 1-57091-884-8 (softcover)
  [1. Dark matter (Astronomy)—Fiction. 2. Astronomy—Fiction. 3. Brothers and sisters—Fiction. 4.
Mystery and detective stories.] I. Title: Dark matter mystery. II. Johnson, Meredith, ill. III.
Title.
  PZ7.L369926St 2006
  [Fic]—dc22   2004027796

Printed in Korea
(hc) 10 9 8 7 6 5 4 3 2 1   (sc) 10 9 8 7 6 5 4 3 2 1

SNAP! Stella Brite popped her bubblegum. Mayor Pickle's Pekingese had been on the loose for a week now. If she could track down that tricky pup, everyone in town would know about the Brite and Brite Detective Agency.

Stella's brother, Max, came running in. He waved a newspaper in her face. "Stella, put the mayor's pooch on hold!" he shouted. "This is the case of a lifetime!"

Can the Dark Matter Mystery Be Solved?

Much of the universe is made of dark matter, yet dark matter remains one of today's greatest mysteries.

What is it? Where is it? Scientists all over the world are trying to solve these mysteries.

"Mysterious missing matter!" Stella exclaimed. "Let's take the case, Max."

She grabbed her detective backpack. "We'll start by doing a routine background check at the library," she said.

She threw some doggie biscuits into her pack. "Just in case," she added.

Doggie TREATS

At the library, Max found a book called *The Universal Encyclopedia of Everything*. "This has got to have something," he said.

"Let's take a look at these, too," Stella said.

Dark Matter Notes
Max Brite, Assistant Detective

Universe: All of the matter and energy that exists.

Later Stella and Max compared notes at Zwicky's Pizzeria. Stella asked, "So what did you find out about dark matter?"

"Matter is anything that has mass," Max said. "I'm matter. So is this pizza. And mass is the amount of stuff in an object." He looked hopefully at the pizza. "If I could have that last slice of pizza, I'd have more mass."

"And a bellyache," Stella said. "Look over there!" When Max turned to look, she hid the pizza under the table.

"I don't see anything," said Max. "Hey! Where'd the pizza go?"

"It's here," Stella said, laughing. "You just can't see it. It's like dark matter. Scientists think dark matter should exist, but they can't find it."

She gave Max the pizza. "We're going to find that matter, Max. And I know where to look." She tapped a flyer on the wall. "The astronomy club meets tonight at Lookout Hill. Let's go!"

Astronomy CLUB

Tonight!
Lookout Hill

Mass: A measure of the amount of material in an object.

Matter: Anything that has mass.

At the top of Lookout Hill, kids were looking through telescopes of all sizes. A tall boy named Ben let Max have a look. Max called out, "Hey, I see Jupiter! And four of its moons."

Ben nodded. "Jupiter is really big, so it has a really strong gravitational pull. Its gravity holds more than 30 moons in orbit."

"So the moons go around Jupiter while Jupiter goes around the sun," said Max. "Does the sun go around anything?"

"The sun goes around the center of the galaxy, just like all the other stars of the Milky Way," answered Ben.

"That must be some powerful gravity that keeps all the stars together," Stella said.

"Actually, that's the funny thing," Ben said. "Based on the stuff we know, there isn't enough mass to hold our galaxy together. The stars and gases on the edges should go flying off into space—but they don't."

Stella blew a big bubble and popped it with a bang. "Galloping galaxies, that's it!" she said.

A photo collage of Jupiter and four of its moons, Io, Europa, Ganymede, and Callisto

Gravity: The force of attraction between two objects. Any two objects will pull on each other. The strength of that pull depends on the mass of the objects and the distance between them.

Galaxy: A collection of stars, planets, and gases. Our galaxy is called the Milky Way.

"Scientists think there's some invisible matter holding together each galaxy, right?" Stella asked. "Well, that could be dark matter!" Max looked puzzled.

Stella pulled out a yo-yo. "Close your eyes," she said. She stepped behind a row of bushes and began whirling the yo-yo above her head. "OK, where am I?"

"You're behind the bushes, of course," Max said. "Oh, I get it! You're like the missing dark matter. I can't see you, but I know you must be there, holding on to the yo-yo."

"So dark matter holds together galaxies," Stella said. "But what is it, exactly?"

Ben shrugged. "I don't have a clue, but there's the person to ask." He pointed to a shadowy figure darting through the trees. "Just be careful," he warned.

Stella and Max looked at each other. The mysterious figure disappeared into the darkness. "Let's tail her!" Stella said. "She must be up to something!"

Stella and Max followed the mysterious figure into a large brick building. In the dim light, they saw a thin woman hurry down the hall and slip into an office. A sign on the door read "Professor Bella Black."

Soon the woman rushed out, leaving the door ajar. "Now's our chance," whispered Stella. "Let's see what—or who—is inside." Max gulped and followed.

The only signs of life in the room were two parrots and a goldfish. "Looks like the coast is clear," Stella said. "Time to hunt for clues. What is dark matter anyway?"

"Wimps!" screamed the green parrot.

Max jumped. "Who're you calling a wimp?" he demanded.

"Machos!" shrieked the red parrot.

"Yeah, you two are tough machos, all right," muttered Stella. "Why don't you birdbrains be quiet?"

13

"Wait a minute," Max said, holding up a book called *The Weird, Wild World of WIMPs*. "Maybe these parrots know something we don't."

The green parrot bobbed its head. "Wimps!" it screeched. Max grabbed another book. "And look at this: *MACHOs and the Hunt for Dark Matter*."

"Machos!" The red parrot squawked.

Max flipped through the book. Suddenly he laughed. "MACHO stands for Massive Compact Halo Object. MACHOs are invisible objects with lots of mass—maybe old, dying stars. They don't give off any light, so it's really hard to detect them. I wonder how people know they're there?"

"I think that's what this picture shows," Stella said, pointing to a diagram on the board. "Here's the MACHO in the middle. Its gravity is bending the light waves coming from a star."

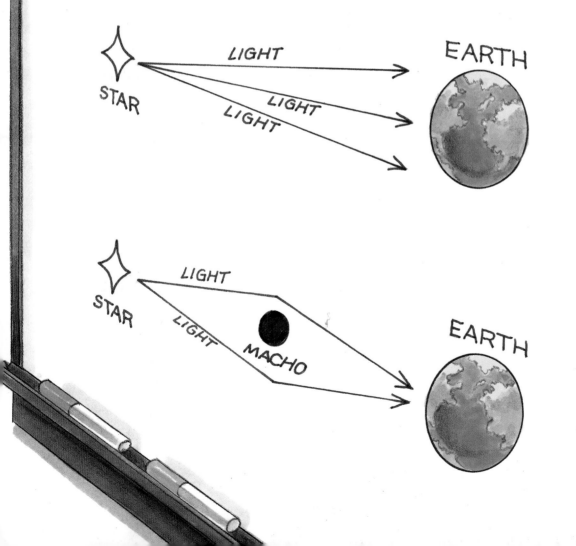

Max looked skeptical. "How can light bend?" he asked.

Stella stepped behind the fishbowl. "Tell me what you see, Max."

Max peered into the fishbowl. Stella and the goldfish peered back at him. "I see you and the fish," he said, "but you look funny."

16

"That's because the fishbowl is curved like the lenses in a pair of eyeglasses. They both bend light waves," Stella said. "The gravity of a MACHO can bend light waves, too."

"It's like you and the yo-yo!" Max exclaimed. "We can't see the MACHO, but we can see what it does to something else!"

"Macho! Macho!" screeched the red parrot triumphantly.

"Shhhhh!" Stella hissed. "Keep it down!"

Stella returned to the picture on the board. "Here you're looking at a star through a telescope. It looks normal.

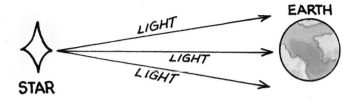

"But suppose a MACHO sits between you and the star.

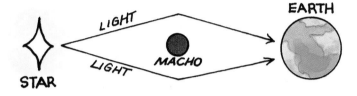

"The starlight bends around the MACHO. Here on earth, we see the bent light rays combined together." Stella chewed her gum furiously. "I can't quite imagine how it would look."

"Maybe it would look like this," Max said, pointing to a poster. "Brighter, because all that light adds up."

"Brilliant detective work, Max!" Stella said. "When the star gets brighter, it's a clue that there's a MACHO lurking about."

Max looked more closely at the poster. "Don't celebrate yet, Stella. This poster says that MACHOs make up only 20 percent of the dark matter in the Milky Way. If that's true, then where's the rest of the dark matter?"

At that moment a scratchy voice interrupted them. "What exactly is going on here?"

Stella and Max gasped and ducked behind a cabinet.
Peeking out, they saw the thin woman talking on a cell phone.
"I scheduled the dark matter hunt for tomorrow morning at
7 a.m. I expect the equipment to be at the old mine by that
time. Please see that it's ready." She hung up and turned
to the parrots.

"And now it's time for you to go to bed, Einstein."
She covered the green parrot's cage with a dark cloth.

"Wimps," came from behind the cloth.

"You, too, Vera."

"Machos," said the red parrot in a muffled voice.

"Good night, Newton," Professor Black told the goldfish. She picked up her briefcase and hurried out the door.

Stella and Max grinned at each other. "Maybe she's not so bad after all," Max said. "She likes animals."

"And she gets up early," Stella added. "I wonder if we can get some pancakes with that dark matter?"

The next morning Stella and Max biked out to the old mine. They hid and waited.

Soon Professor Black appeared, leading a group of sleepy students. "Listen up!" she barked. "We're here to hunt for dark matter particles called WIMPs — Weakly Interactive Massive Particles.

"The hunt won't be easy. WIMPs have a lot of mass, but they're tiny. They are like ghosts that can pass through the entire earth. In fact, hundreds of millions of them are passing through your bodies right now. If they exist, that is."

"What makes you think they exist?" a student asked.

Professor Black held up a picture. "This shows the X-rays emitted by a giant cloud of hot gas 4 billion light-years away. It yields valuable clues about dark matter."

Stella leaned forward so she could see the picture. Suddenly she felt herself slipping.

X-ray: A high-energy form of light not visible to the human eye. Some types of really hot matter, including clouds of gas left over from exploding stars, emit X-rays.

Light-year: Approximately 5,880,000,000,000 (almost 6 trillion) miles. That's the distance light can travel in one year.

CRASH! Stella landed on the ground at the professor's feet. "What is this? Who are you?" Professor Black demanded.

Stella scrambled to her feet and held out her hand. "Good morning, Professor. I'm Stella Brite, of the Brite and Brite Detective Agency. My assistant, Max, and I are trying to solve the case of the missing dark matter."

Professor Black raised an eyebrow. "Stella and Max, eh? This morning my parrot Einstein told me, 'Stella and Max are wimps.'"

Stella turned red, but she continued, "Our apologies for snooping, Professor, but we learned the facts about MACHOs. Now, thanks to your picture here, we understand the evidence for WIMPs."

"We do?" asked Max, coming out of hiding.

Stella explained, "It's like seeing a city from an airplane at night. The X-rays are like the lights on the buildings. But the buildings themselves—the matter holding the lights in place—are invisible."

"An interesting way to put it," Professor Black said thoughtfully.

Stella continued, "And because the glowing gas is really close together near the center, the dark matter holding it in place must be really small. Small, but with a lot of mass—like a WIMP!"

Professor Black smiled. "Exactly," she said.

"Now come with me, everyone," she ordered, leading them into an elevator. "Here on the surface of the earth, we're constantly bombarded by cosmic rays from outer space. These particles would interfere with our experiment, so we use the earth as a filter. It blocks cosmic rays, but lets WIMPs pass through.

"WIMPs rarely bump into anything," Professor Black continued. "But when—and if—they do, we hope to hear them. If a WIMP bumps into one of the atoms of our crystal detector, our instruments should pick up a little 'plink.'"

Cosmic rays: High-energy particles—mostly protons— that travel through space.

The elevator came to a stop. Professor Black led the way into a giant cavern. "And now, ace detectives, welcome to our lab! You can help us look—or should I say listen?—for WIMPs."

Stella and Max listened

and listened

and listened some more.

The day went by without so much as a single WIMP "ping," but Professor Black was cheerful. "WIMPs are elusive, but if they're there, we'll find them! You can come back and help anytime, Detectives Brite."

"Thanks!" Stella said. "This case isn't closed yet, Professor."

As they biked home, Max sighed, "Finding dark matter is a lot harder than I thought."

"Yeah," Stella agreed, "but now we know a lot more about the way the universe works. And we'll stay on the dark matter case, no matter how long it takes. Solving scientific mysteries is a lot harder than tracking down missing dogs, that's for sure!"

"Speaking of missing dogs . . . ," Max said, getting off his bike. "See how that bush is shaking, even though there's no wind? I think I know what's moving it. It's like dark matter: I can't see it, but I can see what it does—" He dove into the bush.

After a brief scuffle, Max emerged holding a small brown
dog. The dog wagged its tail and looked hopefully at Stella.

"Mayor Pickle's Pekingese!" Stella cried, scooping up
the dog. "You pesky Peke! It's a good thing we found you."

She checked her backpack. "Or maybe you found us!"

DARK MATTER

Scientists have been searching for dark matter since the 1970s, when an astronomer named Vera Rubin and others discovered that stars near the edges of a spiral galaxy were moving much faster than expected. The stars were moving so fast that they should have gone flying off into space. The scientists concluded that there must be some kind of invisible matter holding the galaxy together. (An astronomer named Fred Zwicky made the same discovery back in 1933, and even dubbed the missing matter "dark matter," but no one believed him at the time. They thought he was a kook.)

MACHOs: In 1993, astronomers reported seeing a star that temporarily got brighter before returning to its normal brightness. Since then, they have observed thousands of such events. They theorize that this phenomenon is caused by a MACHO, a Massive Compact Halo Object. A MACHO can act like a lens to magnify starlight. As much as 20 percent of the galaxy's dark matter may be made of MACHOs.

WIMPs: Physicists think that most of the dark matter in the universe is made up of tiny particles formed when the universe began. Little is known about these mysterious particles, called Weakly Interacting Massive Particles, or WIMPs.

Scientists really do look for WIMPs deep under the surface of the earth. One experiment, called the Cryogenic Dark Matter Search, runs in an old lead mine in Soudan, Minnesota. Other scientists use NASA's space-based X-ray telescope, Chandra, to figure out where dark matter might be. Some scientists are even trying to manufacture WIMPs in laboratories by crashing particles together.

So far, no one can explain exactly what dark matter is or how it works. Perhaps you will help solve these mysteries!

WEBSITES

To learn what's happening in the search for dark matter, check out these websites:

StarChild: A Learning Center for Young Astronomers
http://starchild.gsfc.nasa.gov

The Chandra X-ray Observatory
http://chandra.harvard.edu/edu